Ollie's Christmas Reindeer

Nicola Killen

SIMON AND SCHUSTER

London New York Sydney Toronto New Delhi

It was Christmas Eve and Ollie had just gone to sleep when

jingle, jingle, jingle

she woke again with a start.

What was that sound?

She rushed to the window, but all she could see was a blanket of fresh snow!

Grabbing her sledge, she ran downstairs . . .

... and stepped out
into the wintry night.

Laughing aloud, Ollie jumped up
to catch a falling snowflake, when
she heard the magical sound again.

Jingle, jingle, jingle.

She had to follow it.

Whooooooosh!

Racing down the hill, she heard the ringing again.

Jingle, jingle, jingle.

And this time it was much clearer.

As the wind whistled and the
trees shook, the bells got louder.

Jingle, jingle, jingle.

Ollie was getting close.

She took a deep breath and, feeling very brave,
she ran into the darkness.

There, hanging from a branch,
was a collar circled with silver bells.

Who could it belong to?

Then came a new sound . . .

Crunch, crunch, crunch.

A reindeer stepped through the crisp snow towards Ollie.

"H... h... hello," she whispered, not quite believing her eyes. "Are you looking for this?"

The reindeer knelt down patiently while Ollie fastened his collar.
Then he lowered himself even further.

Ollie knew exactly what to do and clambered onto his back.
She wondered if they would go for a ride through the forest,
but to her surprise . . .

. . . they soared up into the night sky,
leaving the trees far below!

They travelled over snow-covered
lands and seas glittering in the moonlight.
As they journeyed on, Ollie shivered,
and the reindeer knew there was one last
place he should take her.

The new friends landed softly in the snow.
"Thank you," Ollie whispered.

They didn't want to part, but there was
someone very special who needed the
reindeer's help that night.

Yawning sleepily, Ollie crept back to her room . . .

. . . and was soon dreaming of her magical journey.

Jingle, jingle, jingle.

This time the silver bells didn't wake Ollie . . .

. . . as her reindeer flew
through the night sky
once more.

In the morning, Ollie found her presents.

Now she would always think of her new friend.
"See you next year!" she whispered.